# Boxes! Boxes!

# HANDLE WITH CARE

# BOXES!
# BOXES!

Leonard Everett Fisher

The Viking Press, New York

In memory of my father-in-law
Hyman Meskin
A loving and learned man

"A kind and gentle heart he had..."

—OLIVER GOLDSMITH

First Edition
Copyright © 1984 by Leonard Everett Fisher
All rights reserved
First published in 1984 by The Viking Press
40 West 23rd Street, New York, New York 10010
Published simultaneously in Canada by Penguin Books Canada Limited
Printed in U.S.A.   Printed in Japan by Dai Nippon Printing Company Ltd.
1   2   3   4   5   88   87   86   85   84

Library of Congress Cataloging in Publication Data
Fisher, Leonard Everett.   Boxes! Boxes!
Summary: The boxes in a young child's room are of different
sizes and shapes and used for a variety of purposes.
[1. Boxes—Fiction. 2. Stories in rhyme] I. Title.
PZ8.3.F635Bo   1984   [E]   83-14761   ISBN 0-670-18334-2

A box can be small.

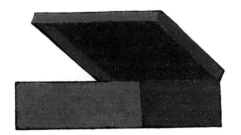

A box can be tall,

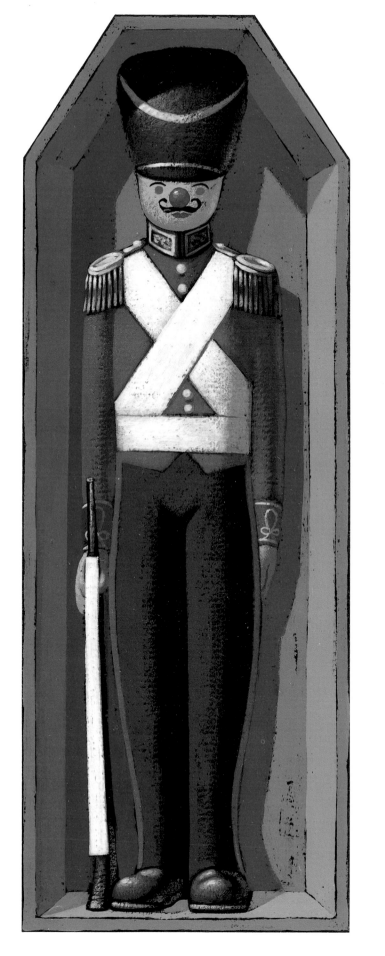

# Narrow and slim

Or filled to the rim.

I have boxes for nesting,

Napping and resting,

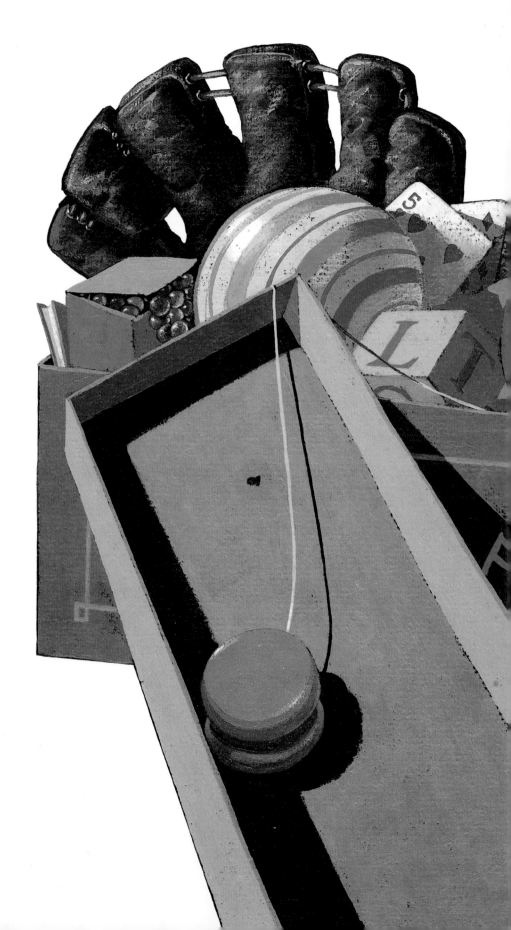

# Sparkling with treasure

And my paints
for good measure.

Box a plant.

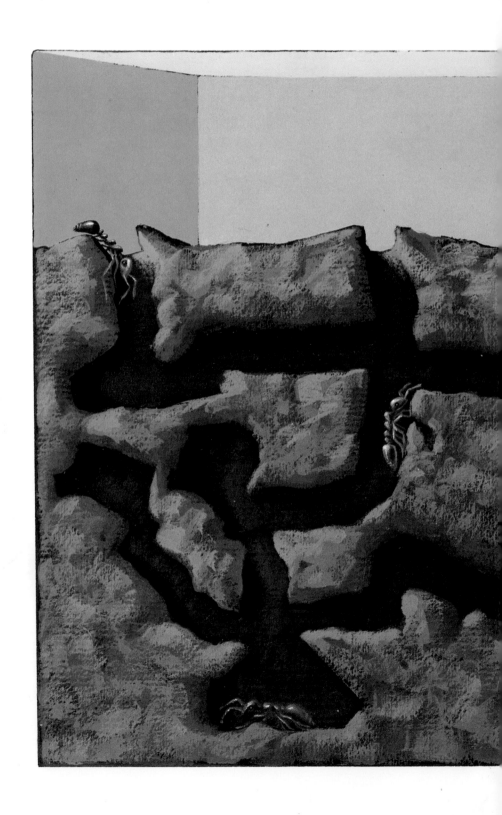

# Find an ant.

Pile them high.

# Look out! They can fly!

They can pop and zoom!

Boxes! Boxes!
All around my room.

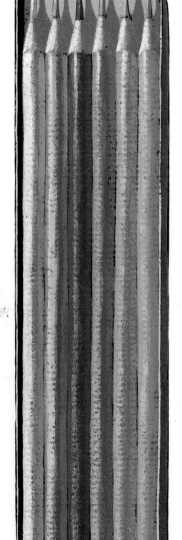

ABOUT THE BOOK

BOXES! BOXES! took more than two years to create, from idea to finished book. My editor, Deborah Brodie, and art director, Barbara Hennessy, spent an afternoon in my studio in Westport, Connecticut. The walls were covered with very large paintings of boxes and shadows seen from various perspectives. These paintings, intended for gallery exhibition, started us thinking about what a box can be.

I used a full-color range of acrylic paint, just like the tubes of paint shown in this book. My brushes are even smaller than those shown. If you look at the ladybug on a leaf in the plant box (and again in the last picture, where it's half that size), you'll have an idea of just how small the brushes had to be.

There are more than 80 boxes pictured in this book. Look around your room—how many boxes can <u>you</u> find?